AMELIA EARHART

YOUNG AIR PIONEER

Written by
Jane Moore Howe

Illustrated by
Cathy Morrison

A hardcover edition of this book was published in 1999.
© 1999 by Jane Moore How, All rights reserved.
Text illustrations © 1999 Patria Press, Inc.
Cover illustrations © 1999 Patria Press, Inc.

Patria Press, Inc.
3842 Wolf Creek Circle
Carmel, IN 46033
Phone 317-844-6070
www.patriapress.com

Printed and bound in the United States of America

10 9 8 7 6 5 4 3 2 1

Text originally published by the Bobbs-Merrill Co., 1950 and 1961,
under the title, *Amelia Earhart: Kansas Girl*, in the
Childhood of Famous Americans Series®. The Childhood of
Famous Americans Series® is a registered trademark of
Simon & Schuster, Inc.

First trade paperback edition published 2000.

The hardcover edition has been catalogued as follows:

Howe, Jane Moore.
    Amelia Earhart : young air pioneer / written by
Jane Moore Howe ; illustrated by Cathy Morrison. —
2nd ed.
    p. cm. — (Young patriots series ; 1)
    SUMMARY: A story of pilot Amelia Earhart's
childhood, family life, education, first flight, and
flying lessons.
    LCCN: 98-85710
    ISBN: 1-882859-02-2
    1. Earhart, Amelia, 1897–1937—Juvenile fiction.
2. Air pilots—United States—Juvenile fiction. I.
Morrison, Cathy. II. Title.

    PZ7.H8373Am 1999   [Fic]
                        QBI98-1655

Edited by: Harold Underdown
Designed by: inari
ISBN: 1-882859-04-9
Original Acknowledgment in Bobbs-Merrill edition:

The author wishes to express her appreciation to Muriel Earhart Morissey for
her great help; to Harcourt, Brace and Company, Inc., for their permission to use
Last Flight and *The Fun of It* by Amelia Earhart and *Soaring Wings* by George
Palmer Putnam as sources of factual information; and to G.P. Putnam's Sons for
their permission to make similar use of *20 Hours, 40 Minutes* by Amelia Earhart.

Contents

1   Amelia Comes to Grandma's House   1

2   James Ferocious   9

3   It's Just Like Flying   16

4   School Days in Atchison   24

5   James Ferocious and the Stagecoach   29

6   The State Fair in Des Moines   38

7   Amelia Goes Exploring   45

8   Christmastime at Grandma's   55

9   Christmas Day   59

10   The New Sled   66

11   Mama Reads Black Beauty   73

12   Graduation   82

13   First Flight   88

14   Flying Lessons   97

15   A Real Pilot   103

What Happened Next?   109

The Mystery of Amelia Earhart   110

About the Author   111

Illustrations

Amelia watched the lightning . . .   3

The big dog was jumping at the ladder . . .   11

Ferocious rushed after the boys, growling . . .   14

"Oh it's grand, it's wonderful!
Why it's just like flying!"   21

In a few moments, the two little girls
came down the steps . . .   31

The dog was growling
and grabbing at the bone . . .   36

As the plane climbed in the air,
Amelia . . . watched it . . .   42

Her foot slipped on a pebble
and she began to slide . . .   51

At last the sled turned
just as she wanted it to . . .   68

Pidge looked around. "Melia,
here comes the milkman!" . . .   78

"It's what I've always dreamed.
I want to fly."   93

Numerous smaller illustrations

To my children,
Jane, Tom, and Addison,
with my love

Chapter 1

Amelia Comes to Grandma's House

The train whistle gave a loud, long toot. Great clouds of smoke blew past the open train windows. Screens kept out the cinders, not the dust and soot. But Amelia Earhart, sitting by the window, didn't care about the dirt. She was busy counting white horses in the farmyards they passed.

"There's another one," she said to Muriel, her little sister. "That makes ten. I wonder how many I'll see before we get there?" Muriel sat across from Amelia, looking out the other window. Her mother sat beside her and Mr. Earhart beside Amelia. It was the summer of 1904, and the Earharts were all going to visit Grandma and Grandpa Otis. Grandpa was a judge in Atchison, Kansas. Grandma kept a large, beautiful house. And the cook, Lilly Bell, always had the best raisin cake Amelia had ever tasted.

"How much longer till we get to Atchison?" Amelia asked again.

"One more hour," said Mr. Earhart, after looking at his big watch. Their father always knew the answers to train questions. He was a lawyer for the railroad and often traveled on trains.

Suddenly, above the clicking of the wheels, they heard the low rumble of thunder. The summer sky was growing darker.

"It looks like a storm," Mrs. Earhart said.

"Yes," said Mr. Earhart. "And this will probably make the train arrive late in Atchison."

Just as Amelia gave a deep sigh, the conductor came down the aisle. He stopped to talk to Mr. Earhart. They were old friends.

"Guess you're traveling for pleasure today?"

"That's right, Mr. Wiggins. We're going visiting. I want you to meet Mrs. Earhart. This is Amelia and this is Muriel. But we call the girls 'Melia' and 'Pidge.'"

"How do you do, Mrs. Earhart," the conductor said. "How do you do, young ladies. We see a lot of Mr. Earhart on this train. It's nice to meet his family." And Mr. Wiggins gave a friendly smile.

"We're not all here," Amelia put in. "Poor James Ferocious has to ride in the baggage car, because he's a dog."

Amelia watched the lightning.
It lit up the whole sky as it flashed.

"That's too bad," said Mr. Wiggins. "But don't worry. The men up there will take good care of him. Tell me," he went on, "where did you get your nicknames?"

Pidge looked shy, but Amelia said promptly, "I'm named for my Grandma Otis. Her papa called her Amelia only when she was bad, and she didn't like it. So she never calls me Amelia—just Melia. That's what everyone calls me."

"Melia named me Pidge," put in Muriel.

"She's always singing 'Little Blue Pigeon,'" Amelia explained. "So I just call her Pidge. I wish she'd learn another song."

"I like to sing 'Little Blue Pigeon,'" said Muriel. "It's by Eugene Field. I'm going to sing it always. Do you want to hear me?"

Amelia looked out the window again. She didn't want to hear "Little Blue Pigeon."

She got her wish. Before Pidge could begin there was a flash of lightning, followed by a loud clap of thunder.

"We'd better put these windows down," Mr. Earhart said. "Stand out in the aisle, girls."

The two men put down the heavy train windows. The porter was also busy closing windows. Soon the coach felt hot and airless.

"You're a tall girl, Melia," Mr. Wiggins said, as he stepped back in the aisle. "And you stand as straight as a soldier—just like your papa."

"I was seven years old last month," Amelia said proudly, "on July twenty-fourth. Pidge is only three and a half. I'm going to stay with Grandma and Grandpa and start school in Atchison."

"I'm going to stay, too," Pidge echoed.

"Why, that's fine." Mr. Wiggins waved good-by and started down the aisle.

Rain started to spatter against the windows. The sky grew even darker. "It's almost as dark as night," Amelia thought.

"I don't like storms," she said aloud.

"Me neither," Pidge said.

"Suppose there's a storm when we're at Grandma's?" Amelia put her hand into her papa's. "I'd better go to California with you."

"But school will begin before we come back," Mama said, "and you won't want to miss that. Think what a big girl you are, starting school."

"I don't care. I want to go with you. I'll miss you and Papa too much."

"Why, Melia, you'll have such fun at Grandma's," said Papa. "You and Pidge would get tired traveling. It's a long trip. I have to go on business and I want Mama to see California."

"I want to see California too," Pidge said.

"You and Melia can both see California when

you're older," Papa said.

"I'd rather see it now," Amelia said. "I don't want to stay in Atchison."

"Grandma's house is big and cool in summer," Mama reminded her.

"And remember how you like to play in the old barn," Papa added.

Another bright flash of lightning lit up the dark sky. There was another deep roar of thunder, and rain poured against the windows. The train seemed to sway on the track.

Pidge began to sob. "I don't like this, Mama!" Her mother put her arm around the little girl.

"There's too much lightning," Amelia said. "Will we have an accident?"

"Oh, I don't think so," Papa said. "You mustn't be afraid, Melia. Remember our family always tries to be brave."

"But I'm not really brave, Papa. I'm afraid of lightning." Amelia hid her face against her father's shoulder.

"My father told me about a great storm like this. He had to travel through it when he came to Kansas before I was born," Papa said calmly. "He and Grandma came in a covered wagon all the way from Pennsylvania, with eleven children."

Amelia had never heard this story. "I'll bet they

were scared."

"Yes, they were. But pioneers had to face danger. They learned to be brave. That day the rain came down so hard it soaked the canvas and leaked into their wagon. It was cold and the wind almost a gale. The horses couldn't see to walk. They had to sit in the rain and wait for the storm to pass."

"Couldn't they get under a big tree?" Amelia asked.

"No, they didn't dare do that, because if lightning had struck the tree, it might have fallen on them. That night they had only a cold supper of leftover corn bread. There was no dry firewood to build a fire. Even their beds in the wagon were wet."

Amelia forgot about the storm. She forgot about the flashes of lightning and crashes of thunder. She thought only about her grandfather and grandmother, traveling from Pennsylvania in a covered wagon.

"I wish I'd been a pioneer. I'd like to travel in a covered wagon."

"Why, you can be a pioneer, Melia," Papa said. "The world is very big. There will always be new things to do. But you must be brave enough to do them. And courage is something you learn each day."

Amelia was quiet for a few minutes. She watched the rain on the windows run down in little rivers of water. She watched the lightning. It lit up the whole sky as it flashed. She listened for the loud rumble of thunder that followed. As they passed a farm she saw a man driving his cows back to a barn for shelter.

"He isn't afraid to be out in the storm," she thought. "And a pioneer girl wouldn't have been frightened. She wouldn't even have minded her papa and mama leaving her for a trip."

Aloud she said, "I don't think I'll be so afraid of lightning again. And I'll stay with Grandma and Grandpa while you go to California."

"That's my big, brave girl." Mama smiled.

"That's my pioneer girl," Papa said. "I'm proud of you."

Soon, the rain fell more gently. The sky grew brighter. The train had passed through the worst of the storm.

The door at the end of the car opened suddenly.

"Next stop, Atchison!" called the conductor, as he walked down the aisle.

"It's time to put on your hats, girls," Mrs. Earhart said, as she smoothed their hair. "Papa will see about the bags and James Ferocious."

Chapter 2

James Ferocious

Amelia stood by the kitchen table watching Lilly Bell mix raisin cake. A fresh summer breeze moved the white curtains at the window.

Grandpa and Grandma Otis' big brick house stood on a high bluff overlooking the Missouri River. It had wide white porches at the front and back. Shady elm trees grew around the house. In the back yard there were fruit trees, a grape arbor, a wood shed, and a big barn with a loft.

"May I put the raisins in?"

"Yes, baby." Lilly Bell gave the cake batter a last good beating. Amelia dropped in the raisins.

"I'm so glad I stayed here with you," Amelia said. "I like to help cook. It's lots more fun than shopping with Grandma and Pidge."

Next she scraped the sweet batter from the bowl.

"When will Papa and Mama get back from California?"

"Not for a long time yet," Lilly Bell answered.

Suddenly, they heard loud, fierce barking and frightening growls in the back yard. Amelia hurried to the window and stood on her tiptoes.

Two boys were teasing James Ferocious, the big black dog, who was tied by a rope to the old elm tree. One ran up close to the dog and yelled. The dog leaped at him. But the rope was too short, and the boy jumped back just in time. The dog ran after him but the rope yanked him back. Then the other boy ran up from another direction and yelled. Up jumped Ferocious. He lunged after this new enemy. Again he was almost jerked off his feet by the rope.

Amelia didn't stop a second to think. Ferocious needed her. He was her dog, her family, just like Pidge and Mama and Papa. She banged open the screen door and rushed into the back yard. "You boys stop teasing my dog!" she called. "It hurts him to jump at you like that!"

The two boys stopped their game. They looked at the angry little girl with yellow pigtails. Then they glanced at the angry black dog.

"Aw, we're just having fun with him," said the larger boy.

"Well, Ferocious isn't having fun," Amelia said. "You're bad boys. And I know who you are, too.

The big dog was jumping at the
ladder and snarling fiercely.

You're Baily Waggoner and Jared Fox."

Jared, the taller boy, jumped toward Ferocious again. The dog leaped—and James Ferocious' rope broke!

Ferocious rushed after the boys, growling deep in his throat. His long black hair bristled around his neck. His sharp teeth showed. He had never bitten anyone, but Amelia felt sure he would bite now.

"Run for the shed roof!" she screamed. "Quick!"

The boys ran. They climbed the old ladder leaning against the shed so fast their feet barely touched the rungs.

Two frightened boys looked down from the roof of the shed. The big dog was jumping at the ladder and snarling fiercely. Amelia had never seen him so angry. Then Ferocious noticed the little girl standing all alone by the tree. He turned and ran toward her. He still snarled, and his teeth showed angrily.

"Run! He's a mad dog. Run!" yelled Baily Waggoner, the smaller boy.

Amelia stiffened. Ferocious was like a mad dog, wild with rage. But Amelia didn't run. She stood perfectly still. "Ferocious knows me," she thought, "and he won't hurt me."

She spoke to the angry dog. "James Ferocious, be quiet. Look what you've done. You've spilled all your water. You know you're supposed to stay here by the tree."

James Ferocious looked back at the boys on the shed roof. He growled again.

"Lie down, Ferocious. Good boy. No one's going to hurt you. I won't let them hurt you." And Ferocious finally lay down at her feet.

She called to the boys on the shed roof, "You'd better get out of this yard and never come back." Then she reached down and rubbed the dog gently behind his ears.

Judge Otis hurried down the back porch steps. His face was pale. Close behind came Lilly Bell. She had run into the living room to tell Judge Otis.

"Melia, honey, are you all right?" he asked anxiously.

"Yes, Grandpa. Those boys were teasing James Ferocious."

"Baily and Jared, go home," Judge Otis said. "And don't ever tease Melia's dog again. It's lucky he didn't bite you."

"Yes, Judge Otis," said two meek little boys. They climbed down quickly and hurried away.

"You were very brave, Melia," said Grandpa. "I'm proud of you. If you'd run from him, Ferocious might have bitten you."

"Why didn't you run, baby?" Lilly Bell asked. "Weren't you scared?"

Ferocious rushed after the boys,
growling deep in his throat.

"Yes, I was scared," Amelia confessed. "But Papa said I had to learn to be brave."

"Well, you used your head, Amelia," Grandpa said. "You were as brave as any little girl could be."

"I'm glad Ferocious didn't really bite those boys, Grandpa." She put her small hand into his big one. "He's big, he could bite awfully hard."

"I don't think they'll tease him again."

Chapter 3

It's Just Like Flying!

Amelia sat on top of the shed, hammering away at a short board laid across the roof. "Pidge, hand me up some more nails."

Pidge jumped down from her seat on a heap of old boards by the shed. She got some nails and started up the ladder. Amelia slid down the shed roof to meet her.

"I think this will be the very best thing we've ever made, Pidge. But there's still a lot of work."

Ferocious was lying half asleep under the grape arbor. Suddenly he growled and got to his feet. Amelia looked up and saw Jared Fox. No wonder Ferocious sounded cross.

"Quiet, Ferocious. Lie down," she said.

"Hello, Melia. I came over to say that I'm sorry I teased your dog. I won't do it again. I brought him a bone."

Jared unwrapped a big steak bone and held it out to James Ferocious. The dog took one happy sniff and relaxed. His tail gave a small thump.

"That's all right. I'm glad he didn't hurt you, anyway." Amelia climbed back to her perch on top of the shed and began hammering again.

Jared stayed and watched Amelia. "What are you making?"

"Oh, Pidge and I are going to have our own rolly coaster. Right here, from the shed." And Amelia pounded another nail. It bent.

"Want me to help?" Jared offered.

"Not really," Amelia replied.

Jared watched a little longer. Finally Amelia scrambled down the ladder. She began lifting a long, heavy fence board.

"I could lift that for you," Jared said. "I'm real strong. I'm eight years old."

Amelia remembered how he had teased her dog. But he had also brought the bone. Finally she said, "Well, I guess you can help. Pidge is pretty small. Our cousins Tootie and Katchie Challis were supposed to help, but they haven't come yet."

Jared grinned. "How'd you ever think of making a rolly coaster, Melia?"

"Pidge and I saw one in Des Moines at the park. Papa wouldn't let us ride on it. He said the cars went too fast."

Amelia climbed back up to her seat on the shed roof. "Jared, you lift up that long board. I'll nail it here for one of the tracks."

Jared lifted. Pidge tugged. Amelia picked up the hammer and a nail. She hit the nail as hard as she could. It bent. She pulled it out and took another nail. The same thing happened.

"I'll do it," Jared said. He climbed up beside her. "See, do it like this. Don't hit so hard at first." And he drove the nail in straight.

Amelia watched him. "You're good. But let me try the next one. I want to learn how."

Amelia held the nail and hit it gently. This time the nail went in almost straight.

Tootie and Katchie Challis hurried into Grandma Otis' back yard. Tootie was just four months younger than Amelia. And Katchie was the same age as Pidge.

They wanted to be in on the fun of the roller coaster. Now that Melia and Pidge were here, there was always something going on. Melia never ran out of new ideas.

"We're late," Tootie said. "But we had to help Mama."

"I want to work on the rolly coaster," said Katchie.

"There's lots to do," Amelia said. "Jared is helping, too. He's strong and can drive nails."

All the children worked hard. They pulled and lifted, hammered and pounded. Finally the track was finished—three long boards from the shed roof to the ground like a big slide. They nailed guard rails on each side to keep the roller-coaster car on its track.

"Now for the car," Amelia said. "This flat little board will be nice. We'll hitch my old roller skates to the bottom for wheels."

"How're you going to make the wheels stay on?" Jared asked.

Amelia turned the skates over and over. That was a problem. "It's only the wheels we really need," she said at last.

"I think they come off," Jared said. "See, they'll unscrew."

"Then we can bend nails over to hold them on," Amelia suggested.

Jared laughed. "You'll be good at driving those nails, Melia."

Amelia laughed too. "Yes, that's what I'm best at—driving bent nails!"

A little later Amelia leaned back and looked with satisfaction on their work.

"That," said Pidge, "is the very best rolly car

I ever saw."

"I'll try it out," Amelia said.

"I'd better go first. I'm a boy," Jared said.

"Pooh! I'm not afraid. Being a boy doesn't make any difference." And Amelia climbed to the shed roof. Jared handed up the little car.

Carefully Amelia got on it. She called out, "Here I come!" And she gave a push.

The little wheels squealed and down she flew. At the end of the track, Amelia turned a somersault and lay flat on the ground.

Ferocious rushed up, barking. Jared and Tootie yelled. Pidge and Katchie yelled too.

"Did it hurt you?"

"Oh, Melia, are you all right?"

"Of course I'm not hurt!" Amelia picked herself up. "It's grand! But the track isn't long enough."

"Aren't you going to quit?" Tootie asked.

"Of course not. We'll just get more boards and make a longer track."

After some more hammering, Amelia climbed up to the roof for her second try. Again she crawled on the car.

"Coming down!"

Almost before she could catch her breath, the little car rolled to a stop at the end of the track. Amelia jumped off.

"Oh it's grand! It's wonderful! Why it's just like flying! I flew!"

"Oh it's grand! It's wonderful! Why it's just like flying! I flew!"

Ferocious caught Amelia's excitement and began to bark. He barked long and loud.

Judge and Mrs. Otis heard Ferocious as they sat on the broad front porch.

"Perhaps we'd better see what the girls are doing," said the judge. "Ferocious is very excited about something."

The two hurried around the house to the back yard. On top of the shed they saw Jared Fox, with Tootie Challis beside him. Jared was sitting on a small board with wheels attached. Pidge and Katchie were climbing up to the roof. Amelia was hammering away on a board.

"What is that thing, Melia? What in the world are you children doing?" Grandma asked.

"Grandma, it's a rolly coaster. It's just like flying," Amelia cried excitedly. "I flew!"

"Flying! I never saw such a dangerous contraption," Grandma said. "You children will break your necks."

"This can't go on. I'll have Moses take the roller coaster down this afternoon," Judge Otis said.

"But, Grandpa," Amelia cried, "we've just finished it!"

Grandpa shook his head. "It's not a good plaything for little girls. You'll get hurt. How you ever made it in the first place is a wonder to me."

"That one ride was such fun," said Amelia. "Please let the others try it just once. It isn't fair. They want to fly too."

Jared and Tootie looked sadly at the roller coaster. There were tears in Pidge's and Katchie's eyes.

"We didn't even get to ride," Tootie said.

"And we worked so hard. All morning!" Jared said.

Grandpa looked sympathetic, but he said firmly, "No, children, I can't let you risk it."

Amelia gave her beautiful roller coaster one last look. After all that work, they would have to give it up. She knew Grandma and Grandpa meant what they said. She whispered softly to the others, "Don't feel too bad about it. We'll think of something else to do."

Chapter 4

School Days in Atchison

Judge Otis' black, square-toed shoes made a pleasant creaking sound on the stairs as he came down to the dining room.

"Good morning, my dear." Judge Otis kissed his wife. He sat down at the big table across from her. "Where are my little girls?"

"They'll be down in a minute," Grandma said. "They're collecting their books."

Grandpa began to open his mail.

With a clatter of feet on the stairs and a noise in the hall, Amelia and Pidge came in.

"Good morning, Grandma and Grandpa."

"Good morning, dears."

"Mmmm, I'm hungry," Amelia said. "I could eat twelve eggs and twenty biscuits."

"I doubt that," Grandma said. "But you can try!"

Grandpa looked up. "I'm pleased with your report

card, Melia. You always do well in English. But I don't understand how you always get A in arithmetic. I never see you study or write out your problems."

"Oh," Amelia said, her mouth full of biscuit, "I do them in my head. It's easier. I thought the third grade would be hard, but it's not."

The girls ate quietly for a time. Soon, Grandma said, "It's time to go to school. And wear your coats. These October mornings are chilly."

The girls kissed Grandma and Grandpa, grabbed their books and went out. Tootie and Katchie came out of their house next door and the four little girls started off to school.

Miss Hall turned the big globe of the world around and around.

"Here we are in Kansas," she said, "right in the middle of the United States."

"Here is Europe," the teacher said, "here the British Isles. Down here is Africa." She slowly turned the globe. "Asia is on this side of the world. And away down under is Australia. Here in the middle of the Pacific Ocean is Hawaii."

"What kind of animals do they have in those places?" asked Baily Waggoner.

"That's what we're going to learn this year in geography," Miss Hall answered. "Also the names of the countries, cities, rivers, and mountains of the world."

"Will we learn about the people, too?" asked Eddie Jackson.

"Not in geography. We learn about people in history. We'll have some of that this year."

"I like to know about people," Eddie said.

"I like to know about places," said Amelia. "I wish I could see some of those countries."

"It's a long way to go," Tootie said. "Kansas looks mighty small on that globe."

"Birds can see it all," said Amelia. "In the air the earth must look just like the map on the globe. I wish I could be a bird for a while."

"Being a bird is a pretty fancy, Amelia," said Miss Hall. "But now there are aeroplanes, you know. They cannot fly so far as a bird, but at least people can fly in them."

"Yes, I could take an aeroplane," Amelia said. "Then I could go to the places that have those wonderful names—Newfoundland, Wales, Hawaii, Africa."

The teacher smiled. "Aeroplanes cannot fly that far, Amelia. But perhaps you will travel to those places anyway."

"Being a bird would be the best way," Amelia said. "They're better at flying."

"Birds can see it all," said Amelia. "In the air the earth must look just like the map on the globe."

The boys and girls laughed. So did Miss Hall. Then the teacher said, "It's time for your English compositions. I want you to write about the subjects we've been talking about this morning."

The children went back to their seats. They got out their tablets and pencils. Some squirmed in their seats and looked out the window. Others chewed their pencils. Then they began to write their compositions.

After a while Miss Hall said, "Time's up. Hand in your compositions."

She glanced through the pile of collected papers and chose one. "Here is one I'll read first. It is very good. This is Amelia's." She began to read:

"I watch the birds flying all day long,
And I want to fly too.
Don't they look down sometimes, I wonder,
And wish that they were me
When I'm going to the circus with my daddy?"

Chapter 5

James Ferocious and the Stagecoach

Amelia hurried to answer the doorbell. She pulled open the big front door. The parcel-post man stood on the porch with a large box.

"Do Miss Amelia and Miss Muriel Earhart live here?"

"Yes. That's me. That's us!" Amelia answered. In her best third-grade writing she wrote "Amelia Earhart" on the slip of paper he handed her. He gave her the big box.

"And there's a letter stuck on top, too."

"Thank you," Amelia said as she closed the door. "Pidge, oh, Pidge! Come quick! It's a box from Mama in Des Moines."

Pidge came running. "I'll get the scissors. Let me cut the string, Melia."

Amelia wondered what Mama had sent. The package wasn't heavy enough for books. Together the girls opened the box. Under the paper wrapping Amelia saw dark blue flannel—things to wear. She lifted the top one. As she held it up she realized what it was.

"Pidge, they're bloomers. How wonderful!"

Pidge held up the next one. "It's a blouse to go with the bloomers." She looked again into the box. "There's a set for each of us."

Amelia pulled the letter off the box and read the note aloud to Pidge. "Mama says here, 'These are for you to wear for play. I'm tired of so many ruined dresses. Have lots of fun in them. Love, Mama.'"

"Aren't they grand, Melia! Our skirts can't blow up."

"And we can climb and jump so much better. Let's put them on right now, Pidge."

The girls gathered up box and bloomers. They hurried to their room.

Grandma Otis returned from a shopping trip in town. She had the cab driver help her bring in a large package. He put it in the front hall closet. She took off her small velvet bonnet. She hung it on the hall coat rack.

"Melia! Pidge! Where are you?"

In a few moments the two little girls came down the

In a few moments the two little girls came down the
steps wearing their new bloomer suits.

stairs, wearing the new bloomer suits. Grandma's eyes opened wide. Her mouth opened wide. She looked again at the bloomers. They were pleated.

Grandma seemed to grow two inches taller. "And where did you get those?" she asked.

"Mama sent them," Amelia answered. "They just came. Aren't they lovely?"

"Lovely is not the word. Why in the world would your mama send those pants? No girls wear such things."

"She said they were for us to wear for play. She's tired of ruined dresses," Amelia explained.

"Well! My granddaughters will not wear pants. You both go put on your plaid dresses and embroidered pinafores."

Amelia looked down sadly at the new bloomers. She touched the soft blue flannel. Pidge put her hand into Amelia's for comfort. There were tears in her eyes.

"Now, dears, you are both so sweet and pretty," Grandma said coaxingly. "You look so nice in your dresses. There's not a boyish-looking thing about either of you."

"We don't want to look like boys, Grandma," said Amelia. "But skirts get in our way when we play. I like pretty dresses, too, when I'm dressed up for a party."

"Well, you won't be doing anything that a dress can't do," Grandma said. "Go change your clothes and come back. I've brought you both a present from town."

Amelia and Muriel went slowly back up the stairs. Only the thought of Grandma's present kept back their tears.

In a little while they came down again. Their plaid dresses had long sleeves and white collars. Their white muslin pinafores had bands of eyelet embroidery trimming. Their crisp sashes were tied in butterfly bows. And there were big plaid hair bows on their pigtails.

"Now that's the way little girls should look," said Grandma in a pleased voice. "Come and see what I've brought you!"

She brought out the big package from the hall closet. The girls tore off the paper. It was a wicker doll carriage.

"Why don't you take your dolls for a ride?"

"Thank you, Grandma," Pidge said.

"Yes, thank you very much, Grandma," said Amelia.

Pidge picked up a doll and put it in the carriage. The two little girls pushed the carriage out the front door. Then they slowly rolled the carriage around to the back yard.

"I wonder what we should do with it?" Amelia said. "Wheel it around like little ladies and keep clean, I guess."

"We could play dolls," Pidge suggested.

"That's not much fun."

"Nope."

"There ought to be some good use for it," Amelia said. "I wish we could have worn our new clothes, anyway." She thought again. "Let's play 'Stage-coach'!"

"We don't have a horse."

"There's James Ferocious!"

Hearing his name, the big dog came down from the back porch. He wagged his bushy tail.

"How can you hitch him to the carriage, Melia?"

"That's easy. We'll make a harness out of rope from the barn. I think I saw some leather trunk straps there, too."

In the barn, the girls rummaged around in the dusty toolroom until they found the rope and straps. Cobwebs clung to their hair. Dirt smudged their hands and faces and streaked their starched white pinafores. But neither one noticed. They hurried back to the little doll carriage.

Pidge looked at their collection in wonder. "How can we ever make a harness out of that?"

Amelia didn't stop to answer. She was busy tying

knots and fastening buckles. Pidge watched, her eyes wide. James Ferocious watched, his eyes sleepy.

"See, Pidge? This will go around his head. Here are the reins. This fastens to the doll carriage— I mean stagecoach."

"Oh."

"Here, Ferocious, nice doggy. Let me harness you up," Amelia said.

James Ferocious stood up. He let the harness be tied and the doll carriage be hitched.

"Giddap, Ferocious. The mail must go through!"

Ferocious looked around at Amelia. He didn't giddap. He didn't growl or bark. He just lay down and rolled on his back.

"Melia, he won't play."

"Now, Pidge, don't give up so easily. You go to the kitchen and slip out that bone Lilly Bell saved for Ferocious' supper. It's on the table."

Pidge set off. Amelia worked on the harness. Big old Ferocious still lay like a kitten. Then Pidge came back at a run with the bone.

"This is what we'll do, Pidge. I'll tie this string around the bone. You run ahead of Ferocious. He'll smell it and run after you. I'll drive the stagecoach."

Ferocious took one sniff at the bone, and got to his feet at once.

"We're off, Pidge! Giddap Ferocious!"

The dog was growling and grabbing at the bone.
And the brand-new doll carriage was almost flattened.

Away went the stagecoach. Pidge held the bone just ahead of Ferocious' nose and ran as hard as her legs would go. Amelia hung onto the reins. The doll carriage twisted and lurched dangerously on its wheels. James Ferocious went after his dinner.

Around the house the stagecoach traveled. Ferocious barked and ran. Amelia yelled, "Giddap, giddap! Here comes the mail!" Pidge didn't yell. She just ran.

In front of the house, Ferocious gave an extra hard pull, and the harness broke. Ferocious leaped for the bone. Down went Pidge, the carriage turned over, and Amelia landed on top of Pidge, Ferocious and the doll carriage.

The front door opened and Grandma came out. She was just in time to see the mix-up. The two little girls' pinafores were torn, their dresses were dirty, and their faces were smeared. The dog was growling and grabbing at the bone. And the brand-new doll carriage was almost flattened.

Grandma Otis put her hands to her head. She shook it sadly. "I hope you're not hurt," she called to her granddaughters. Then she added, "Your mama was right. Go and put on the new bloomers. I'm tired of ruined dresses, too!"

Chapter 6

The State Fair in Des Moines

"**H**appy birthday, Melia!" Pidge shook her sister's shoulder.

Amelia opened her sleepy eyes. She saw the wallpaper with roses in it and for a second she couldn't remember where she was. Then she remembered. She was ten years old and she and Pidge were with Mama and Papa in Des Moines.

"Let's hurry and get dressed." Amelia ran across the room to her clothes, which lay neatly folded on a chair. "Isn't it fun living with Mama and Papa for the summer?"

"Yes, but I wish the railroad company didn't make Papa move so much," said Pidge. "Or I wish we didn't have to go to school and could travel with them."

Amelia laughed. "I like the second wish better!" And Amelia began to sing:

"I went down south to see my gal,
Singing Polly wolly doodle all the day."

"You sound mighty happy," Pidge said.

"I am. We're with Mama and Papa. The State Fair is here in Des Moines. We're going. And best of all, it's my birthday and I'm ten years old!"

The merry-go-round whirled around and around. The horses went up and down. Amelia and Pidge waved at Papa each time they passed. He stood beside the ticket seller's booth. He had stood there for the last two rides.

"That's the last time, girls," he called. "Let's go and see the new aeroplane. We've never seen one."

"Just one more ride, Papa, please," Amelia begged. "Remember it's my birthday."

"Not now. I want you to see the aeroplane. We'll have to hurry—it's going to rain soon." He led them through the crowds.

Amelia stopped suddenly and stood perfectly still. "Papa, ponies! We have to ride the ponies. We might not find them again."

Mr. Earhart sighed. "But I want you girls to see the aeroplane. It's a wonderful new invention. The first aeroplane flew only five years ago."

"Yes, Papa," Amelia said patiently. "But these are live ponies. We could ride them."

"Please, Papa," added Pidge. "Remember it's Melia's birthday."

Papa gave up. He followed the girls to the pony track. "Two tickets, please." He laid the money on the counter.

Amelia and Pidge mounted two tired little Shetland ponies. They started a slow walk around the dirt track. Amelia clucked to her pony and gave him a slight dig in the ribs with her heels. The pony speeded up into a slow trot. Amelia bounced along with Pidge close behind. They came back to the starting point much too soon.

"Can we ride again, Papa?" Amelia asked. "It was so much fun!"

"We are going to see the aeroplane before it rains," Papa said. Amelia knew it was his "I-mean-business" voice.

Sadly, Amelia and Pidge climbed down from the ponies. Taking their father's hands, they trailed along, looking at the wonderful sights of the fair. They came to a field with a high wire fence. Inside was a higher wooden fence. A large sign at the gate said FLYING AEROPLANE.

"It's about to rain, Papa," Amelia objected. "Shouldn't we get under a tent?"

"We are going," said Papa, "to see the aeroplane. I want to see it even if you don't."

Amelia had no more to say. She gave the sky another look and then followed her father through the gate to the flying field.

A strange object made of wood and wire stood in the center of the field. Amelia looked it over. It had two wings, one above the other. There was a small seat in the center between the wings. A man perched there like a bird on a branch. The tail of the plane looked like a box kite. There was a motor just behind the man. As Amelia watched, it began to make loud sputtering noises. A helper gave a wooden board a turn and it began to whirl. Amelia thought it looked like a pinwheel.

"Now watch, girls. It's going to fly!" Papa said excitedly.

The plane slowly rolled over the field on its small wheels. It rose from the ground.

"See, it flies!" Mr. Earhart watched closely. "It's heavier than air and yet it flies."

As the plane climbed in the air over the field, Amelia forgot the ponies and the rain and watched it. It looked like a strange bird.

"It would be fun to be a man and fly one," Pidge said.

"I don't see why a girl couldn't fly one, too," Amelia said.

"I don't suppose they'll ever have any practical

As the plane climbed in the air over the field, Amelia
forgot the ponies and the rain and watched it.

purpose," said Papa, "but they're a great scientific
discovery."

As the aeroplane circled above the field, the rain
came. The plane headed down. It landed and rolled
to a stop. The crowd rushed for cover. Mr. Earhart
hurried his daughters to the near-by grandstand.

"You have seen a wonderful thing," he told them. "Not many people have seen an aeroplane. I hope you will always remember it."

"Will it fly again today, Papa?" asked Amelia.

"If the rain stops. But we'd better go home."

"Let's wait and see it fly again," Amelia begged.

"Did you hear the whir of the engine? Did you see the wings tip like a bird's?"

Papa looked at her in surprise. "For a little girl who would rather ride the ponies, you've changed in a hurry, Melia."

"I just didn't understand about aeroplanes. I didn't know they would be so exciting. I'd rather see it than anything else at the fair."

Chapter 7

Amelia Goes Exploring

Amelia put the little garter snake back into the cage. She was very proud that she had found it for her museum on Grandma Otis' back porch in Atchison. There was a big garden toad in a box with two grasshoppers, red spiders in a bottle, and colored pebbles on the window ledge.

Tootie and Katchie Challis and Ginger Parks, Amelia's school friend, stood watching.

"Let's play a game," Ginger said. "I don't like that old snake."

"Let's play 'Boogie' in the barn," Amelia suggested.

"What's that?" Ginger asked.

"Oh, it's a good game," said Katchie. "Melia named it that."

"Come on," Pidge said. "We'll show you."

"I'll race you to the barn," Amelia shouted. She

45

ran down the steps.

The four other girls dashed after her. They opened the big door and headed straight for the old carriage. Grandpa still kept it, though now he had no horses. The girls climbed up on the dusty seats.

"What do we do now?" Ginger asked.

"We go traveling," Tootie explained.

"Let's go to Washington, D.C.," Amelia said.

"What's at Washington, D.C.?" Pidge asked.

"Why, that's the capital of our country. There's a lot to see and do in Washington, D.C."

"Oh, yes," Ginger said. "Miss Hall was telling us about it in school yesterday."

"There's the Capitol Building," Amelia said. "See the big dome on top!"

"There's the Smithsonian Institution," added Tootie. "Miss Hall says there are animals there."

"Can we shoot them?" Pidge asked.

"Of course not, silly!" Amelia said. "They're stuffed. Besides, we're going sight-seeing, not shooting."

"There's the White House." Ginger pointed.

"Let's stop and have dinner with the President of the United States," Amelia suggested. "He lives here."

"Whoa," Pidge said obediently to the make-believe horse.

"Why, we can't just stop in and have dinner with

the President," said Tootie. "That's a crazy idea, Melia."

"They wouldn't even let us in the front door," Ginger added. "He's a very important man. He wouldn't bother with you."

"Maybe someday he would," Amelia said stubbornly. "Grandma says I have very nice table manners."

"It will take a lot more than table manners to see the President," said Tootie.

"I'm tired of sight-seeing," said Pidge.

"Me too," said Katchie. "This isn't like a game. It's like school."

Amelia wasn't having a very good time either.

"Papa showed us an aeroplane last summer at the Iowa State Fair," she said. "Let's make-believe we're in an aeroplane. We could fly far away. We could fly to England, maybe."

The other girls laughed. They all knew an aeroplane couldn't fly all the way across the ocean.

"Let's go play 'Pioneers,' Melia," begged Pidge. "It's lots more fun."

"Papa says there are lots of ways of being a pioneer," Amelia argued. "He says someday there will be air pioneers."

"Well, you'll never be one," Ginger said. "A girl could never fly an aeroplane."

"Girls can do anything that boys can do. I'm sick

and tired of being told I can't do this and I can't do that. And all because I'm a girl!"

Amelia felt angry now. She was tired of "Boogie." She was tired of the girls laughing at her. She was tired of being told she couldn't do things when she knew that she could.

"I can drive a nail as straight as Jared Fox can," she said. "I can hit a baseball as well as Baily Waggoner…well, almost. And my museum collection is better than any boy's in my class. I'm sick and tired of playing with you girls. You think you can't do anything. I'm going on a real adventure. And I'm going all by myself!"

Amelia climbed down from the carriage. She walked out of the barn and she didn't look back.

Amelia walked behind the barn to the edge of the bluff. She scuffed her feet through the few fallen leaves. She stopped and looked at the Missouri River, far below, and the trees, now red and yellow.

Amelia wished she could go down the little path that ran down the side of the bluff to the river. But that was against all Grandma's rules. And so was exploring the caves in the side of the bluff or playing by the river. Grandpa and Grandma were afraid they'd meet a bad tramp, or fall in the river. Boys could do all those things, but girls couldn't.

She had told the girls she was going on a real adventure. She decided this would be a very good place to start. Amelia started down the little path. Partway down she saw a large sign next to the opening of a cave. In big black letters it said BEWARE.

"Now here's an adventure," Amelia thought. "What's in the cave? Who put up that sign?"

She climbed across the side of the bluff, holding on to bushes and a few small trees. She reached the cave and went in.

It wasn't very large. Near the opening were two large rocks and Amelia could see that a campfire had once been built between them. She wondered who had camped there. A tramp? There was no one here now. She could see no reason to say BEWARE.

She came out of the cave and looked down the bluff. Something moved on a bush below her and caught her eye. Amelia looked closer. It was a moth, a big moth. She crawled down the bluff, hoping for a fine addition for her museum. She crept up to the moth quietly. Carefully she picked it off the bush. It was a beauty with large pale-green wings. She felt sure it was a Luna.

Amelia felt much more cheerful now. This was a real treasure. She knew that Luna moths were rare. Baily had one in his collection, but this was the first live one she had ever seen.

For a while she stood examining and admiring the moth. Finally she started back to the path. But her foot slipped on a pebble and she began to slide down the steep bank. She held the moth with both hands to protect it and tried to dig her feet into the earth. That slowed her a little. Then she slid into a clump of low bushes. She was so relieved to crash into them that she didn't mind the scratches.

Amelia got up carefully. She examined the moth. It seemed to be all right, too. Then she looked about her. "Why, I've slid over halfway down the bluff!" she thought. "And I've found another cave behind these bushes."

She pushed back the leaves and went into the cave. It was much larger than the one by the path. It was quite deep, too. Amelia explored it. She kept hearing water dripping and bubbling.

As her eyes grew used to the dim light she could see a spring. It bubbled up in a rock basin. Amelia went over and dipped her fingers into the water. She felt a small loose rock and pulled it out. She took it to the cave opening to see it better. It was an Indian arrowhead.

"Talk about the boys having adventures!" she thought. "I'll bet Jared and Baily will wish they'd been with me!"

Her foot slipped on a pebble and she
began to slide down the steep bank.

Amelia carefully put the arrowhead into her pocket. She looked at the Luna moth in her other hand. It no longer fluttered. She wrapped it in her handkerchief and put it in her pocket too.

She heard someone coming down the path. Amelia started back to the cave to hide, but she was too late. Her cousin, Jack Challis, Tootie's and Katchie's big brother, had already seen her.

"What are you doing down here?" he called. "Don't you know everyone's been looking for you for over an hour?"

"I'm exploring," she answered, trying to say it as calmly as, "I'm having oatmeal for breakfast."

"You know you're not allowed to play on the bluffs," Jack said. "Come over here right now. I'm going to take you home."

"I can go home by myself," Amelia said. But she crawled meekly across the bluff to the path.

"What do you know about exploring anyway?" Jack laughed. "You belong up at the house with the girls."

"Well, I found a Luna moth," Amelia said, "and guess what else I found!" She reached into her pocket and brought out the arrowhead. "See! I found a cave with a spring, too."

"You were lucky," said Jack. "But you're going home now."

"Did a tramp put up that sign saying 'Beware'?" asked Amelia as they climbed back up the steep path.

"Did that scare you?" Jack laughed. "Some of the boys did that for people like you!"

"It didn't scare me at all. That's where I found the Luna moth."

"It had better scare you off next time," Jack said. "You're really going to catch it at home."

"You're being a tattle-tale," she said angrily.

"Oh no, I'm not. I'm looking out for you. You're my cousin and I don't want you to get hurt."

Amelia didn't have any more to say. She knew Jack was right. And she wasn't looking forward to seeing Grandma, Grandpa, and Mama.

"Here she is, Grandma," said Jack. "I found her in a cave down on the bluff."

"Amelia Earhart!" Grandma Otis exclaimed. "You know you're not allowed to go there."

"Yes, Grandma," Amelia said, "but I told the girls I could do anything a boy could do. They made me so mad. I had to show them."

Mama came into the living room. So did Grandpa. They both looked sternly at Amelia.

"I found a Luna moth and an Indian arrowhead," Amelia said weakly. She took them out of her pocket and laid them on the table. She hoped to give the grownups something nice to think about. Her plan didn't work.

"There are rules you must obey for safety," Mama said. "Since Papa isn't here to do it, I guess it's up to your grandpa to punish you."

"Come along, Melia," Grandpa said. "I raised your mother by the rule 'Spare the rod and spoil the child.' I think it's a good rule for you, too. We'll get a switch from the woodpile."

Chapter 8

Christmastime at Grandma's

Afire burned brightly in the fireplace. It lit the Otises' big living room with a rosy glow. A cold December wind made the shutters rattle. Grandpa rocked gently heel-and-toe with his back to the fire. His black boots made a pleasant squeaking noise.

"That's a very cozy sound," Amelia thought. She got up from her big chair. She put down her book and joined Grandpa before the fire. Her head now came almost to his shoulder.

"I don't believe Christmas will ever really come." She began to heel-and-toe, heel-and-toe, just like Grandpa. Her shoes made only a small squeak.

"Just one more week, Melia." He smiled at her. "It will come. Have you answered your papa's letter? You'd better tell him what you want for Christmas."

"I've been thinking. I'm trying to decide what I

want the very most. I think I'll ask for—Oh, there's the doorbell. I'll bet it's the girls. They went to get the Christmas greenery."

Amelia ran to the door. She let in Tootie, Katchie, and Pidge.

"Look at the big wreath, Melia." Pidge held it up proudly. "See all the little pine cones?"

Tootie and Katchie laid down their bundles of holly and pine boughs.

"I'll show Grandma the wreath," Pidge said. "Then I'll hang it on the door."

"We got some corn to pop and string for the tree," said Tootie.

"And some cranberries, too," Katchie added. "Enough for both your tree and ours."

"I wish I could've gone with you," Amelia said. "My cold is really almost gone, but Grandma kept me in."

"Melia," called Grandma from the kitchen door. "Make Ferocious come in there."

"He likes the smell of your cooking, Grandma." Amelia laughed. "So do I!"

"He gets in the way," Grandma answered. "I see you girls have a busy afternoon planned. If you get through in time you can help me make Christmas cookies."

"I have so many fun things to do today!" Amelia

She began to write. "Dear Papa. . . ."

said. "It's hard to choose." And then she was quiet a minute. "You go on with the decorating. There's something I have to do first—and it can't wait."

Amelia went to Grandpa's big desk. From a drawer she took a sheet of paper. She picked up a pencil and chewed it thoughtfully for a moment. Then she began to write.

December 18, 1908

Dear Papa,

It's nearly Christmas. Soon you and Mama will be here. The turkey is in the barn getting fat. Pidge, Tootie and Katchie are stringing cranberries and popping corn for the Christmas tree.

You asked what I want for Christmas. I've been thinking. I have plenty of baseballs and bats. What I really need the most of all is a football.

Love,

Amelia

Amelia folded the letter. She put it in an envelope, licked the flap, and sealed it tight. She addressed it. "I'll put it out for the mailman right now," she thought. "Maybe Grandma won't understand why I need a football, but Papa will."

Chapter 9

Christmas Day

"**M**erry Christmas! Merry Christmas!" Amelia called as she came into Mama's and Papa's room.

"Merry Christmas!" echoed Pidge gaily.

The room was still dim with early morning, and the air was frosty with December chill.

"We've come to get our stockings." Amelia hurried to the fireplace. She unfastened her long, black cotton stocking. She felt its bulges. "Look how full it is, Pidge!"

Pidge didn't answer. She was busy getting her own stocking.

Mama sat up sleepily. "You should wait until the house is warm. It's not even daylight."

"I know, Mama, but it's Christmas!" Amelia said.

"You girls hop back into bed. Take your stockings with you," Papa said, "and don't get up until half past seven. The house will be warm then." He yawned, turned over, and closed his eyes again.

Amelia and Pidge ran back to their room.

"I'm cold. Are you, Melia?"

"Yes, but—oh, there's a banana in the top of my stocking! What's in yours?"

Pidge put in her hand. "A banana, and here's an orange."

Amelia reached deeper into her stocking. "There's candy, nuts, cookies, and an apple."

"I'm so glad it's Christmas!" Pidge said happily. "I'd like Christmas every week."

"I wonder what we'll get under the tree. I hope Papa got my letter in time."

Amelia bit into her big, polished red apple.

"Why can't it hurry and be seven-thirty?" added Pidge, as she peeled her banana. Her mouth was already full of candy.

"Now just a minute, girls," Papa said. "We've almost finished breakfast. We always go in to see the tree together."

"Eating breakfast is such a waste of time on Christmas morning!" said Amelia impatiently.

Grandpa came back from a private trip into the living room. Amelia guessed he had lighted the candles on the Christmas tree.

"Shall we all go in now?" he asked.

Amelia and Pidge didn't need another invitation. They ran to the living room and pushed back the big sliding doors.

In the big front window stood a tall, green Christmas tree. Its tiny candles burned brightly. Looped from branch to branch were ropes of tinsel and strings of cranberries and popcorn. Colored balls, twisted glass icicles, and candy canes covered the tree. Beneath the tree were the surprises of Christmas—packages of all shapes and sizes. Amelia's and Pidge's eyes shone like the Christmas star on the tree's tiptop.

"There's nothing as beautiful as a Christmas tree," said Amelia, her gray eyes dancing. "When can we open our gifts?"

"Here's one right on top with your name," Grandpa said. He handed her a white package tied with red ribbon.

Amelia read "To Melia from Grandma" on the tag. She unwrapped it eagerly. It was a square little wicker box with a hinged top. "A fishing box!" she squealed.

"No, Melia," said Grandma, "not that. Why don't you open it?"

Amelia unfastened the small metal clasp and looked inside. The box was lined with tufted blue satin. In the side pockets were spools of thread.

"I didn't expect a football in a flat box. It has
to be blown up, that's all!"

There were packages of needles and pins, scissors,
and a thimble. It was a sewing box. Amelia tried
hard to look pleased.

"I thought you might learn to sew if you had your
own box," Grandma said.

"Maybe I will, Grandma." But Amelia doubted it.

"Now here's a box for you, Pidge, and another just
like it for Melia." Grandpa handed out two more
packages.

"It's from Mama," said Pidge, reading the card.

"A striped taffeta Sunday-school dress! It's lovely, Mama." Amelia held the dress up.

"They match," said Pidge, opening her box. "Look at the velvet collar and cuffs."

"Thank you, Mama," said Amelia.

"May we wear them today?" said Pidge.

"Yes, dear," Mama said.

"Another package, Melia. Merry Christmas to you." Grandpa handed Amelia his gift.

"A book, Grandpa!" Amelia said. She read the title. *"Black Beauty.* It's about a horse. Oh, Grandpa, thank you."

Amelia watched the others open their gifts. She couldn't see Papa's gift. She looked under the tree. There were still some small packages and there was one great big box. She wondered about that.

"'For Melia from Papa,'" read Grandpa. He gave her a flat box.

Amelia looked at it sadly. It wasn't big enough for any football she had ever seen. She slowly untied the ribbon, took off the paper, and opened the box.

"Papa, Papa, you got my letter in time! I thought this was something else. I didn't expect a football in a flat box. It has to be blown up, that's all!" Amelia gave a happy chuckle.

Grandma sat a little straighter. She pulled her

black wool dress over her neatly crossed ankles. She straightened her high lace collar. She didn't say a word, but Amelia knew what she was thinking. Amelia knew Grandma would never have asked for a football if she were a little girl. She wouldn't want one.

"Now for this great big box," Grandpa said. He pulled it from its place at the back. "Let me see," he said. He read the card. It said: "For my two girls to learn the fun of coasting 'belly-whopper.' With love, Papa."

Amelia and Pidge guessed what was in the box. But they couldn't be sure until they looked.

"It is, Pidge! It really is a sled."

"Two sleds, Melia, one on top of the other."

They pulled the sleds out of the box.

"Steel runners, Pidge! Steel runners!"

"A real guide bar in front, too! See?"

"Papa, you always make us happy!" Amelia exclaimed. "This is a perfect Christmas!"

And she looked happily around the room at her family. There sat Grandma, shaking her head.

Grandma spoke. Her voice was quiet but firm. "What's wrong with the old sleds with the wooden runners? All the other girls sit up straight when they coast. Those are boys' sleds."

"These are safer," Papa said, "and they're more fun!"

Amelia went to her grandmother's side. "You can go so much faster on these, Grandma," she explained. "And you really can steer them. Grandma, I do like my new sewing box. I'll try to learn to sew if you want me to learn. I do love you so much."

"I love you too, Melia," Grandma replied. "After all, you are named for me. I hope you will enjoy all your gifts. You already had baseballs, bats, and bicycles. Now you have a football and a boy's sled. I am used to girls being brought up as girls, but it doesn't matter. I'm glad that you're happy."

Amelia smiled. She did want her grandma to be happy. "We'd better put on our new dresses, Pidge. Tootie and Katchie will be over soon for their presents. Let's be dressed in our Christmas dresses."

Chapter 10

The New Sled

Soon after lunch a few days later the doorbell rang loudly. "Someone's in a hurry," Amelia thought, as she ran to answer it. It was Jared.

"Hi, Jared! Come on in. It's cold!"

"Get your sled, Melia," Jared said as he stepped in. "We're going to the big hill to coast. It's frozen solid. Tell Pidge—and hurry." Jared rubbed his hands to warm them. "Tootie and Katchie are going too."

"Hooray! We'll be ready in a minute. Go in by the living-room fire and warm up."

Amelia called to Pidge as she ran upstairs. "Get your warm clothes on, Pidge. We're going coasting on the big hill!"

The three children walked down the snowy street, dragging their sleds, their boots crunching in the dry snow. At the big house next door they yelled, "Tootie, Katchie!"

The Challis girls ran out. They grabbed their high wooden sleds and hurried down the walk. Katchie looked enviously at her cousins' new sleds. "Can I have a ride on your sled, Melia?"

"Sure, Katchie. I'll be happy for you to try it."

The elm trees along the street were all bare. Their branches were frosted with snow. The group walked along and at last they reached the top of the big hill. Most of the children of Atchison were there.

"Hello, everybody!" Jared shouted.

"It's really cold today!" Ginger Parks stamped her feet and rubbed her hands to keep warm. Behind her lay her wooden sled.

"I've never seen the hill this slick," Pidge said.

"Neither have I," said Amelia, "this will be fun!"

Baily Waggoner flopped down on his sled, pushed off, and started the long ride down.

"Whee! Look at him go," Tootie yelled.

"Have you tried it, Ginger?"

"No, Melia, I'm afraid. I can't steer my sled very well. I wish I had one like yours."

"You can't stop once you start today," Amelia said.

"Going to try it?" Jack Challis asked.

"Of course." Amelia put down her sled, lay down "belly-whopper" style, and cried, "Somebody give me a shove!"

Jared gave her sled a strong push. It started

At last the sled turned just as she wanted it to, and she put her head down close to the sled and held her breath.

slowly but soon gained speed. The wind blew sharply in Amelia's face. Her eyes watered, but it was fun! "It's like sailing through the air," she thought, as she flew over the ice. Faintly she heard a warning yell from her friends at the top of the hill.

68

"Look out, Melia! Look out!"

As she looked up she saw a horse and wagon driving out from a side road near the bottom of the hill.

At the top of the hill, Pidge jumped up and down. "It's the junkman!" she yelled. "Stop him!"

"Can't! He's deaf! He can't hear us!"

"She'll be killed!" Tootie screamed.

And Amelia knew that she could not stop. She was too near the horse and wagon. She pushed on the front guide bar with all her strength. She prayed that the sled would turn just a little. She pushed harder. At last the sled turned just as she wanted it to, and she put her head down close to the sled and held her breath.

"She made it!" Pidge let out her breath in a sigh of relief.

"Right under the horse! Between his front and back legs!" said Jack Challis.

At the foot of the hill Amelia looked back. The junkman's horse was plodding on down the road. "I don't think they even knew I was there!" Amelia thought. "He didn't even look, and he knows this hill is used for coasting." She started back up, dragging her sled.

Baily, part way up the hill, waited. "You're lucky to be alive, Melia. That scared me."

"The junkman knows we coast here," Amelia said crossly. "I know I'm lucky. It scared me to death, too." They climbed up the hill.

At the top her friends were waiting quietly.

"We thought you'd be killed, Melia," said Pidge. She grabbed her sister's hand.

"We couldn't do anything," Jared said. "He couldn't hear us yell."

"We were all so frightened!" Ginger said.

"Let's go home, Melia." Pidge turned her sled around. "You couldn't pay me to go down the hill now."

"You're right, let's go," Amelia answered. "You all come home with us. Grandma will give us hot chocolate."

Amelia's and Pidge's friends sat by the fire. Grandma Otis sat with them, too. They all had hot chocolate and cookies.

"You would have been proud of Melia, Mrs. Otis," said Jared. "She did the one thing that could save her."

"How horrible it could have been! I'm thankful Melia is alive and unhurt."

"She always knows what to do," Baily said.

"I would've been too scared to think," said Tootie.

"I was just lucky," Amelia said modestly.

"You weren't just lucky. I'm mighty glad Papa gave us those boys' sleds," said Pidge.

"That sled saved you, Melia, but I still don't understand girls doing the same things as boys in the first place." Grandma shook her head. "The things that your papa and mama let you do have caused plenty of talk in Atchison."

"I know, Grandma, but someone has to pioneer the way for girls," said Amelia. "It might as well be

Pidge and me."

"I guess you are as much a pioneer, Amelia, as the women who settled Atchison."

Amelia smiled lovingly at Grandma. That was a wonderful thing to hear—and coming from Grandma, too!

Chapter 11

Mama Reads *Black Beauty*

"Y̶ou girls hurry and get ready for bed," Mama said. "And I'll read you some more of *Black Beauty* while you drink your milk."

"Goody! Goody!" Pidge said.

"You can bet we'll hurry," said Amelia. "I'm so glad you're here for a visit."

"Stories sound so much better when you read them to us," Pidge added.

As they came back to the living room in their night-gowns and warm robes, Amelia whispered to Pidge, "Drink your milk slowly. Mama said she'd read while we drank. She didn't say how long we could take."

The girls sat at Mama's feet in front of the fire. Once in a long time they took tiny sips from their glasses of milk.

Mama opened the book. "Remember where we were? The little horse, Black Beauty, had been broken to wear a saddle and bridle." Mama began to read. The girls sipped their milk very, very slowly.

"His master was good to him," Amelia interrupted at last.

Pidge nodded. "And I like the little pony named Merrylegs."

"So do I," Mama said. "Drink your milk, girls." She read on in the book. She read on and on. There was still milk in the glasses.

"It's sad Black Beauty was sold to a master who used a checkrein," Amelia said. "What's a checkrein, Mama?"

"It is a rein from the bit in the horse's mouth to the saddle of a harness. It pulls a horse's head up," Mama explained.

"Why did they use them?" Pidge asked.

"It was considered stylish for a horse to hold his head high. But it is very uncomfortable for the horse. In time it ruins his health."

"Do they still use checkreins, Mama?" Amelia asked.

"Yes, dear. I'm sorry to say they do."

"But if it hurts the horse, why do they do it?"

"People still want their horses to hold their heads high," Mama said. "They don't think of the horse's comfort."

Amelia took another sip of milk—a small one.

"That's a bad thing!" she said.

"Poor Black Beauty!" Pidge said sympathetically. "The checkrein made him foam at the mouth. It hurt his neck, too."

"I've seen some horses here in Atchison foam at the mouth," said Amelia. "It must be because they wear checkreins."

As Mama went on, Amelia grew angrier and angrier at Black Beauty's treatment.

"The poor horses. They can't do anything but suffer!" she cried.

"No," said Mama. "They have a hard life if they have an unkind master." She looked at her watch. "Something's going to be done about you girls going to bed! Melia, you have taken one hour and a half to drink one glass of milk!"

Amelia laughed. "You know what you said, Mama. You'd read until we finished our milk."

"Finish it right this minute, young lady. It's long past your bedtime. I won't make such a rash promise again."

Amelia and Pidge kissed Mama good night. They started upstairs to bed. On their way Amelia said, "Pidge, tomorrow we're going to help the poor horses here with checkreins."

Amelia and Pidge rode their bicycles up one street and down another, looking for horses with

75

checkreins.

"There's the Mills Grocery wagon," said Pidge, "in front of the Waggoners' house."

"Come on! Let's go!"

The two girls rode up beside the heavy wagon. The horse's mouth was white with foam. His head was high. His neck was arched.

Harold, the grocery boy, lifted down a large box from the back of the wagon.

"Harold," said Amelia, "just look at your horse. He can't pull that heavy wagon with his head so high. Please loosen the checkrein."

Harold stopped a minute. "That's not my horse. He belongs to Mr. Mills. He put on the checkrein. It's not up to me to take it off."

"The horse would pull much better if he could let his head down," Amelia argued.

"Listen to me, Amelia Earhart," said Harold angrily, "Mr. Mills has the best grocery in town, and he has to have a smart-looking delivery wagon, too. He doesn't want his delivery horse to drag his head and eat everybody's grass. You girls get along. I don't have time to argue."

Amelia and Pidge got back on their bicycles. Amelia said, "Pidge, we won't waste time arguing next time. Come on."

The girls rode off. They didn't stop to talk to anyone. Amelia was looking for a horse without a driver.

"There's the milkman's wagon. He's up at the house delivering milk. Hurry, Pidge!"

The girls got off their bicycles and rushed to the horse. His sides were heaving. His head was so high it was hard for him to breathe.

"We'll do this ourselves," Amelia said.

She climbed up on the wagon shafts, and pulled hard on the tight buckle of the checkrein. At last the strap loosened and slipped out. The horse's head dropped. He shook his head gratefully and stretched his neck.

Pidge looked around. "Melia, here comes the milk-man! We'd better go!"

The girls grabbed their bicycles, but the milkman had seen them.

"What have you done to my horse?" he yelled.

Amelia didn't stop to answer. Neither did Pidge. They rode down the street as fast as they could pedal. Looking back, Amelia saw the milkman hurry into the wagon. He whipped his horse. He was coming after them! They headed for home.

The milkman wasn't far behind when the girls rode into the front yard. They hastily leaned their bicycles against the iron reindeer standing on the lawn and ran to the back yard.

"We'd better hide," Amelia said. "And quick! Get

Pidge looked around. "Melia, here comes
the milkman! We'd better go!"

under those laundry tubs!"

The big tin tubs were turned upside down on the
back porch. Each girl crawled under a tub just in
time. Up the back porch steps stomped the milkman. He pounded on the back door. Lilly Bell came.

"I want to speak to Mrs. Earhart," he said in a big, loud voice.

"Yes, sir," Lilly Bell said. "I'll get her."

Mrs. Earhart came to the back door.

"I've come to see you about your girls," he said angrily. "I'm going to take the kid that let down my nag's head to jail. She'll learn to quit fooling around

79

with what ain't hers."

"Now just what happened?"

"I caught her unbuckling the checkrein of my horse."

"I don't know where the girls are," Mrs. Earhart said, "but I'm sorry they bothered your horse. They were only trying to be kind."

"Kind!" said the milkman.

"Yes," Mrs. Earhart said. "A checkrein hurts a horse. I'm sure you'd get more work out of your horse if he could lower his head a little." She glanced over at the laundry tubs. Under the edge of one there was a black shoe showing.

"I'd never thought about getting more work out of the horse," the milkman said. "He does tire quickly."

"Try it without a checkrein," she suggested.

"Well, maybe," the milkman said. "But you see that your girl leaves my horse alone."

"I will. I promise you it won't happen again."

The milkman left. Then Mrs. Earhart spoke. "Children, I know you're hiding under the tubs. Come right out."

Amelia and Pidge crawled out. Amelia looked at Mama. Mama didn't look angry. Amelia felt better.

"Now, girls," Mama said, "you meant no harm. However, you must mind your own business. After this you are not to uncheck a single horse."

"But, Mama, what about the poor horses, if we don't? Just talking to the drivers doesn't work. We tried that."

"I'm sorry for the horses, too, Melia," said Mama. "But the horses belong to other people. It is very wrong to touch anything that isn't yours."

"Will the horses always have to suffer?" Pidge asked unhappily.

"Someday things will change, I think," Mama said. "More and more stores are getting the new automobile delivery carriages. In time they may take the place of horses."

"I'll be glad when they do," Amelia said, "since I can't help the horses."

Chapter 12

Graduation

The 1910 class of College Preparatory School of Atchison, Kansas, waited in the hall of the school building. It was June, and the weather was very hot. The girls twisted and turned. The boys shuffled their feet. Both girls and boys whispered and giggled. Miss Sarah Walton walked up and down the line.

She stopped beside Amelia. "Are you sure you and Ginger are ready with your poem?"

"Oh, yes, Miss Walton," Amelia assured her. "We're ready. We won't make a mistake."

"Good. I'm counting on you girls. The poem will be an important part of our program. You have been a good student, Amelia. I will be sorry to lose you. But you did not work hard enough on your arithmetic. You could have won the arithmetic honors award, but you didn't spend the time on your homework."

"I don't mind not getting it, Miss Walton. I hope

Together, Amelia and Ginger began to recite.

Ginger wins it. She always works so hard."

There was music in the auditorium now. They stopped shuffling and whispering and marched in. Amelia looked around the crowded room and saw her family. Amelia sat in the front row of chairs between Tootie and Ginger. The exercises began.

The nice rector, Reverend Francis White, made a short speech. There was a song, and then the program said, "Recitation by Amelia Earhart and Virginia Parks."

83

As the two girls walked up on the platform, Amelia suddenly felt nervous and frightened. There were so many faces—rows and rows of people—all watching her. Amelia felt her throat tighten. Her heart was beating so hard she was sure her classmates in the front row could hear it.

She reached the center of the platform. She glanced back at Ginger. Ginger looked as though she were going to run right off the stage and out of the auditorium. Quickly Amelia said, "We are going to recite Thomas Babington Macaulay's poem, 'Horatius' from *The Lays of Ancient Rome.*"

She took Ginger's hand and together they began to recite. And as they went from verse to verse without any mistakes, Amelia began to enjoy the recitation.

They came to their favorite stanza:

"Then out spake brave Horatius
    The Captain of the Gate:
"'To every man upon this earth
    Death cometh soon or late.
    And how can man die better
    Than facing fearful odds
    For the ashes of his fathers
    And the temples of his Gods.'"

They went on easily through the lines they had practiced so long. The audience listened closely to every word. When the girls finished, everyone clapped loud and long. Amelia felt very happy. She and Ginger had remembered all of the seventy stanzas. They had not missed a single one of the five hundred and eighty-nine lines. They had not stumbled over any of the long, difficult Latin names.

As they went back to their seats, Miss Walton whispered to Amelia, "I'm very proud of you both. I thought the poem was too long to learn and recite. But you did it beautifully."

Next came the annual awards for honor work. This was a great moment. No one really knew who would win.

Reverend White stood up. He cleared his throat and straightened his glasses. Then he finally looked at his paper and began to read.

"For outstanding work in history—Edward Jackson."

Eddie went up to get his prize. The rector handed him a package. It looked like a book.

"For excellence in science—Baily Waggoner."

No one was surprised at this award. Baily had always led the class in science.

"For outstanding work in arithmetic—Virginia Parks."

Ginger looked at Amelia in surprise. "I really thought you would win," she whispered. She went up for her prize.

Amelia looked over at Grandpa. She knew he had thought she would win this award. She felt sorry she had disappointed him.

"For excellence in English composition—Amelia Earhart," read Reverend White.

Amelia jumped. Had the rector really called her name?

Tootie poked her. "Go on, Melia. Go get your prize!"

In a daze Amelia walked up on the platform and took the package Reverend White handed her. Back at her seat she unwrapped it. It was a beautifully bound copy of *Macaulay's Lays of Ancient Rome.*

Now came the diplomas. Lucy Challis' name was called first. Then Reverend White said, "Amelia Earhart."

Amelia went up for her diploma. She shook hands with the rector. She said, "Thank you," and went back to her seat.

She watched her classmates go up as each name was called. She felt a little sad. She wouldn't be going on with them to high school. She was going to live with Mama and Papa all the time now.

Soon she would be leaving Grandma's big house on the bluff. It had been fun to live in Atchison— the games, the parties, the sports, the winter sledding. She would be glad to be with Mama and Papa, but she was sorry to be leaving her friends.

The last diploma was handed out. Then the class stood up and sang the school song. Amelia had graduated from grade school. She hurried to show her family the prize.

Chapter 13

First Flight

Ten years later, school days in Atchison seemed very far away. Home now was not Kansas or Iowa or any of the other states Amelia had known as a little girl. Mama and Papa had moved to California.

One afternoon Amelia and her father were sitting on the porch of their house in Los Angeles. She had been home from college only a few days.

"California's beautiful, Papa," she said. "I'm glad I'm through school and can be here with you and Mama."

"So am I, Melia. You had a very mixed-up school life. Going to six high schools in four years is a record. And then the World War came along and upset your college years."

"Papa, I never would've been happy staying in college during the war. I really enjoyed being a volunteer nurse in an army hospital. And there wasn't anything else to do to help.

"The only good thing that came out of that awful war was the aeroplanes. I spent all my free time at the flying field. That was the most thrilling sight in the world. I'll never get tired of watching planes roar up into the air and sail away like great birds."

Papa smiled and said, "You're twenty-two now, Melia. You need to decide what you're going to do."

"Yes, I know I should. But there are so many things I want to do. I like sports, I like to travel, and I like to write. Best of all I liked working with motors in that automobile mechanics course I took. And how can I do all those things?

"But right now, Papa, I noticed in the paper that there will be an air meet at Daugherty Field near Long Beach on Sunday. I'd like to see the planes flying again. Let's go."

"Sure, let's go. I remember our trip to see that aeroplane at the Des Moines Fair."

Amelia looked around the field with interest. She saw the old war planes, Jennys and Canucks, and also the new Army and Navy planes—Douglasses, Martins and Standards. Some were bombers and some pursuit planes, but all were small, with only two seats in the cockpits.

The crowd pushed against the ropes lining the

field. It was hot and very dusty. Amelia didn't notice that. She stared at the pilots in leather coats and helmets. She watched the busy officials hurrying about.

"Don't you think we've seen enough?" Mr. Earhart asked hopefully.

"Why, Papa, it's going to last all afternoon. We can't go now."

"I was afraid of that." Mr. Earhart's collar was limp. His face was smeared with dust and he looked unhappy.

But Amelia eagerly watched the plane flying above the field, doing stunts. It went into a barrel roll—rolling over, over, over. . . .

"Papa, let's go behind the ropes. See that man with a badge saying 'Official'? I want you to ask him how long it takes to learn to fly."

The two crawled under the ropes. Mr. Earhart walked over to the man Amelia had pointed out. Amelia waited. At last her father returned.

"I found out," he said, "that it usually takes between five and ten hours, but it's not always the same for every student."

"How much would lessons cost?"

"You didn't say you wanted to know that." Mr. Earhart went back. Amelia could scarcely wait.

"He says about a thousand dollars." Mr. Earhart

reported when he came back again. "That's a lot of money."

"Papa," Amelia said very seriously, "I want to fly."

Mr. Earhart looked at his daughter in surprise. He paused before he answered her. "Well, I don't think one flight would hurt you. I never heard of a woman flying, but you might as well try it once."

"Oh, Papa, will you arrange it? Do it right away, please!"

Again, Mr. Earhart went back for another talk with the official.

"Papa thinks one flight is all I want," Amelia said to herself. "But it's not. I want to learn how to fly a plane myself. I know now. That's the one thing I want to do more than anything else."

Mr. Earhart returned again.

"It's all set," he said. "You'll have a short hop tomorrow at Rogers Airport."

"Papa, that's the best thing you've ever done for me!"

The California morning was bright and clear. Amelia and Mr. Earhart went to the airfield early. Amelia glanced around curiously. Several planes were on the field.

A pilot came toward them and said, "My name's Frank Hawks. Are you Mr. Earhart?"

"Yes, and this is my daughter." Mr. Earhart shook

the young man's hand. "I arranged for a flight yes-terday."

"Yes, the plane is serviced, checked, and waiting," said the pilot. "It's a good clear day too."

Mr. Earhart nodded politely. Aside, he whispered to Amelia, "It wouldn't be good enough for me ever."

"If you're ready now, Mr. Earhart," said Frank Hawks, "we can take off right away."

"I'm not flying," Mr. Earhart said in a hurry. "My daughter's the one who wants to fly."

"Oh," said Hawks. He didn't look happy.

Amelia saw his expression. Then she smiled. "Why," she thought, "he's afraid I may be frightened and jump out or something. He doesn't trust a woman in a plane. How silly!"

"Come on," the pilot said to Amelia, "if you really want to go up. You'll have to climb up on the wing. It's a big step in a skirt."

"I can manage." And she did.

"There are goggles and a flying helmet on the seat. You'd better use them."

Amelia put them on. Hawks climbed up on the wing beside her and fastened her safety belt.

Amelia looked around the cockpit. There were so many controls. Here was a straight stick. There on the floor were pedals. Across the front panel were dials and gauges.

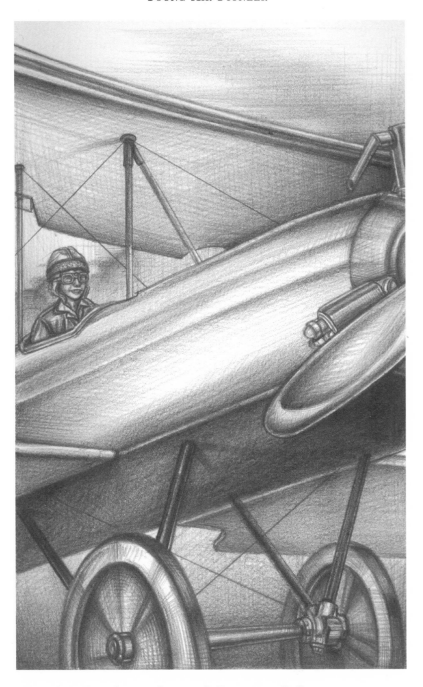

"It's what I've always dreamed. I want to fly."

"What are these things?" she asked.

"That's the stick," said the pilot. "The rudder's on the floor and there is the instrument panel."

"What are they all for?"

"When you pull back on the stick, it brings the nose of the plane up. When you push it forward, the nose goes down. Pull it to the left, and your left wing will dip for a turn. To the right, and your right wing goes down for a right turn," he explained.

"And the rudder on the floor?" Amelia asked.

"That controls the tail rudder. It's like a rudder on a boat and you use it along with the stick to make turns."

"There's a lot for a pilot to learn."

"Sure you're not scared?" Hawks asked.

"Not a bit."

He climbed into the front cockpit and adjusted his helmet and goggles. Then he called to the mechanic, "Brakes! Contact!"

The mechanic gave the propeller a turn. The motor began to hum, the propeller to spin. The wind blew in Amelia's face as the plane began to taxi across the field. The motor made a very loud noise. The pilot turned the plane onto the runway so its nose faced into the wind.

The plane stopped. Amelia heard the motor give a louder roar. The plane started again. It rolled faster and faster down the runway, and soon they were off the ground.

Up, up, up, the little plane climbed. Its nose was pointed above the skyline. Then the plane leveled off. The left wing dropped a little and they turned toward the left.

Amelia noticed the stick moving toward her. Yes, the plane was climbing again. She looked down. Everything was toy-sized—houses, train tracks, and trees seemed small enough for a small doll's playthings.

"I'm free as a bird," she thought happily. "It's what I've always dreamed. I want to fly. I have to learn to fly. I simply have to learn."

The plane made another banking turn. Now its nose was gently pointed down. Amelia noticed that the stick had moved forward. The houses grew a little larger. The plane made another gliding turn, still headed down. The ground was much closer now.

They approached the field, touched down on the runway, and rolled across the ground. Frank Hawks taxied the plane back across the field. He stopped almost where they had started.

Mr. Earhart hurried over to the plane. "How was it, Melia? Were you frightened?"

"No, of course not, Papa." Amelia took off her helmet and goggles. "It was wonderful! I loved it. I want to learn to fly a plane myself."

"When do you start?" Mr. Earhart asked in his best teasing voice.

"Don't laugh. I mean it. I was never more serious in my life." Amelia climbed out of the plane. Her skirt certainly was in her way. "I'll wear breeches after this," she said to Frank Hawks. "And thank you so much for the ride."

On the way home her father said, "Now, Melia, I've never discouraged you from doing the things you wanted to do. But flying is different. It is dangerous, very new, and not suited for a woman. And it is very expensive."

"Papa, I bet they said those very same things to the first women who traveled west in covered wagons. They went ahead anyway and so will I."

Chapter 14

Flying Lessons

Amelia waited patiently until Papa finished his roast beef, potatoes, and beets. When ice cream and homemade chocolate cake were before him, she brought up an important subject.

"Papa, I've made plans for Neta Snook to give me flying lessons," she said in a very calm voice.

"What!" Papa put down his spoon in a hurry.

"I'm going to learn to fly. You remember I told you I wanted to fly."

"You did fly, Amelia Earhart, two weeks ago!"

"But I want to learn to pilot a plane. I've already talked to Neta Snook."

"Who is this Neta Snook?" Mama asked.

"She's a pilot," Amelia explained, "and she gives lessons. She was the first woman to take up flying after the war. She is the first woman pilot to graduate from the Curtiss School of Aviation."

"Well, woman or man," asked Papa, "just who is going to pay for these lessons?"

"I thought you might, Papa."

"A thousand dollars to teach you to fly an aeroplane! Why, I couldn't possibly afford it, even if I wanted you to learn."

"But I want to learn, Papa. I simply have to learn."

"I'm sorry, Melia, but I can't give you that much money."

Papa got up from the table and sat down with the evening paper. The subject was closed as far as he was concerned.

"I'm sorry, too, Melia," said Mama. "But that is a great deal of money. I'm afraid you'll have to give up the idea."

Amelia began to clear the dishes from the table. She would just have to figure how to get money for lessons.

"Young lady," said the man in the employment department of the telephone company, "have you had any experience?"

"No," Amelia admitted, "but I'm awfully anxious to learn."

"Learn what?" the man asked.

Amelia thought of a plane flying across the sky, then coasting down into a beautiful three-point landing. She quickly answered, "Oh, I want to learn all about the telephone company."

"Well, the only thing open now is a job sorting the mail in the back office. I don't know if you'll like working with the office boys. Not many do."

"I will," Amelia said eagerly. "When do I start and on what day do I get paid?"

The man smiled. "You may start today. You'll be paid a week from today."

Amelia looked around the back office. There were stacks of mail and rows of cubbyholes on the wall. Willie, one of the office boys, was matching letters with the names over the cubbyholes. Joe, the other office boy, was opening another sack of mail.

"This is all you have to do," Joe said. "Just read the name and stick it in the right hole. It doesn't take any brains."

"Yeah," Willie said. "It's a perfect job. You don't even have to think."

"Just sit down in that chair," Joe said. "You can watch us for a while. We'll teach you."

Amelia went over to the chair and sat down to watch. But when she tried to move, she couldn't. She was stuck to the chair! She tried to get up. She was still stuck.

Joe and Willie doubled over with laughter. "We

fooled you!" Joe said.

Amelia jerked hard. She got up. A big piece of sticky fly paper came with her. It had been tacked to the seat, and now it was stuck to her.

"That was a good one." Willie laughed. "You'll have a hard time getting it off your dress. It's the stickiest fly paper we could buy."

Amelia had to laugh too.

By the end of the day, Amelia had put stacks of letters into rows and rows of cubbyholes. Outside, it looked as though it would rain forever. But by next week the rain surely would be over, and she would have a pay check—and a flying lesson.

The five o'clock bell rang. Willie and Joe jumped into their rain boots, pulled on their raincoats, and darted for the door.

"Bye, Melia," Willie yelled. "See you tomorrow."

"We have to keep our record," Joe said. "We're always the last ones in and the first ones out. See you tomorrow." And out he ran.

Amelia smiled. Those rain boots had given her an idea.

It was still raining the next morning. Amelia was sorting mail. It was just as Willie had said: she didn't really have to think about it. Now and then she glanced at Joe and Willie, keeping an eye on

She was stuck to the chair! She tried to get up.
She was still stuck.

them. Finally the boys collected a batch of mail and
left the office to deliver it.

Quickly Amelia took a small hammer and some
tacks from her purse. Willie's and Joe's rain boots
were near the door, headed out, ready for their five
o'clock run. Amelia carefully tacked each one to the
floor. Then she put the hammer and tacks back
into her purse and went on sorting mail.

The day passed as the one before had, a letter
here, a cubbyhole there. Every so often Joe or Willie

would collect a batch and deliver them.

Five o'clock came. The bell rang. Joe and Willie went into their usual act. On went the raincoats, they jumped into their boots and they both fell flat on their faces!

"Ha, ha, ha," Amelia laughed. "I fooled you that time!"

Joe and Willie got up. They looked at Amelia in surprise. They looked at their feet, and they laughed. They slipped out of their nailed-down boots and went over to Amelia.

"Welcome, pal." Joe stuck out his hand.

"You can give it as well as you can take it," Willie said.

"I hope you stick around awhile," Joe said.

"I'll be here awhile," Amelia said. "It's going to take a lot of paydays to pay for what I want."

Chapter 15

A Real Pilot

The alarm clock went off at 5:30 in the morning. Amelia turned over in bed and shut it off. On top of her nightgown she wore a shiny new patent-leather flying coat. Her bedroom door opened and Mama came in.

"If I don't get up when you do, I hardly see you all weekend. Now why in the world are you wearing that flying coat in bed?"

"Real flyers don't have such shiny coats, Mama. It looks too new, so I'm trying to get some wrinkles in it. I've worn it three nights now."

Mrs. Earhart laughed.

"Mama, it's taken a long time, but I think I'm going to solo today."

"Do you feel ready?"

"Oh yes."

Amelia got out of bed and began to dress. She put on her breeches and high boots.

"I wish you didn't have to wear those," her mother said.

"The field's dusty and it's hard to climb in and out of planes." Amelia picked up her leather jacket and leather helmet. "Everyone wears clothes like these. A skirt just gets in the way. I'd like to cut my hair short, too. It would be so much easier. But people think I'm strange enough being a woman flyer."

Amelia kissed her mother. "You go back to bed, Mama. I'll get something to eat. And when I get back tonight, I'll have done my solo!"

Amelia took the hour's ride to the end of the trolley line. Then she started the long walk down the highway to the airfield. As she hurried along she thought back over her flying lessons.

She remembered her first lesson with Neta Snook.

"You must learn the parts of the plane," Neta had said, "and their uses, before you try to fly."

Neta had showed her the wings, the ailerons on the wings, the tail rudder, and the propeller. Then they had climbed into a little dual-control training plane and studied the stick, the rudder, and instrument panel.

When Amelia knew the plane perfectly, Neta had taken her up into the air. The first time, she watched Neta control the plane as they circled the field.

Amelia remembered how fast her heart beat when Neta said, "Now you take the controls." She had tried to do just as Neta had done, but it wasn't easy to keep the plane level. At the slightest touch on the stick or rudder the plane dipped or turned.

Next she had learned turns. She practiced right and left turns, climbing and diving turns, over and over. The hardest thing of all came after these—the takeoffs and landings. They still were hard.

The day that Neta had said, "We're going to try some stunts today," had been an exciting one. Amelia knew she had to learn these. Not to show off in the air, but to get her plane quickly back into a normal position if the plane got into trouble. She had practiced slips, stalls, and spins until she knew instantly what to do next.

And after Neta Snook had sold her plane, Amelia had taken more lessons from a new teacher, John Montijo. Last weekend he had said, "I think you're ready to solo now."

Amelia had been anxious to hear those words. Now that the time had come, she wondered if she really was ready. "Up in the air alone," she thought, "I might forget all I've learned."

When she reached the airfield, she almost wished she was back home in bed. But not for long.

She saw her teacher waiting by the training

plane. "Ready for your solo?" he asked.

"Yes, John—if you think I know enough."

"Sure you do."

Amelia quickly crawled into the open cockpit. She didn't want to lose her courage. She didn't stop to check over her plane. She could think only of taking off alone, with no one beside her to help in case of trouble.

She adjusted her helmet and goggles. She put her feet on the rudder bar. "I must remember," she thought, "this makes the plane turn." She took the stick in her hands. "And this makes the nose go up or down and the wings bank." A boy who had soloed last week had been so excited he had forgotten those first simple lessons. At last Amelia called, "Switch off. Contact!"

John gave the propeller a spin, and it began to turn. Amelia taxied across the field.

Facing into the wind on the runway, Amelia stopped the plane. She raced her motor to check both magnetos. She looked at each dial on her instrument panel to see that it was working properly. "Here I go!" she thought, as she started the plane moving.

The plane rolled across the runway. She pulled back on the stick and the nose lifted off the ground. The plane began to rise. But something was wrong. The left wing sagged.

"What have I done?" she wondered. She didn't

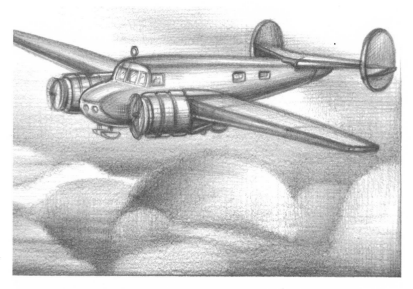

"It's the most wonderful feeling in the
world—up in the sky alone. . ."

dare go on. She pushed the stick forward. The plane
came back to the ground and she taxied to a stop.

John Montijo and some watching flyers came running.
"What's wrong?" John yelled.

"I don't know," Amelia called. "It's the left wing.
It won't lift." She climbed out of the plane, laughing nervously. "It was a short solo."

A mechanic crawled under the wing. "The shock
absorber is broken," he said. "I'll fix it."

Amelia walked over to the hangar with the men
to wait. "I'll never again take off in a plane without checking everything myself," she thought.

At last the mechanic finished the repairs. This time the plane climbed steadily.

"That wasn't bad," she thought. The plane went up, up, gaining altitude. She felt her ears pop. She swallowed hard. The wind blew against her face. On she climbed. Without stopping to think how, she made a left climbing turn. She leveled off at five thousand feet.

"I'm flying," she thought, "and I'm flying alone! I'm not one bit afraid. It's the most wonderful feeling in the world—up in the sky alone, flying through snowy clouds. There's nothing like this."

Amelia made a diving turn. She leveled off, then went into a glide headed down toward the landing field. The solo take-off and flight had gone well, and now she faced the problem of landing. She came down over the runway, ready for the landing. "It must be on three points," she thought. "The two front wheels and the tail wheel must land at the same time."

But the plane bumped when it hit the ground. "I didn't do it right. It wasn't a three-point landing. And I've practiced so many times!"

John Montijo ran out to meet her. "You did it!" he called. "You were fine, except for that rotten landing!"

"I know," Amelia said. "It was bad. But I've soloed! That's the big thing! Soon I'll have my license, and then I'll be a real pilot!

What Happened Next?

1928   Amelia became the first woman to fly across the Atlantic Ocean as a passenger.

1932   Amelia flew solo across the Atlantic— the first woman to do so.

1935   Amelia was the first person to fly alone across the Pacific Ocean from Hawaii to California.

The Mystery of Amelia Earhart

On May 20, 1937, Amelia and her navigator, Fred Noonan, took off from Oakland, California to begin a record-breaking flight around the world. Somewhere between New Guinea and Howland Island, their plane disappeared. Nine naval ships and more than 66 airplanes searched the area but never found a trace of Amelia, Fred or the plane.

Some say Amelia was on a secret government mission and was captured by the Japanese. Others say that she and Fred landed on Gardner Island instead of Howland Island and camped there waiting for help that never arrived. Many people have tried and are still trying today, but no one has yet solved the mystery of Amelia Earhart. What do you think happened?

About the Author

"How could I write about Amelia Earhart going up in a plane for the first time if I had never experienced it?" explained Jane Moore Howe, former newspaper columnist and author of Amelia Earhart, Young Air Pioneer. "So I went to the airport (this was 1949 mind you!), took my first plane ride in a tiny training plane and landed with my stomach doing flip-flops. Then I knew how Amelia must have felt."

Mrs. Howe's concern for detail while writing *Amelia Earhart* also resulted in a long friendship with "Pidge," the aviator's sister, whom Jane consulted regarding the incidents included in the book. "I wanted to choose events that showed Amelia's courage," Jane said.

The first edition of *Amelia Earhart* was published in 1950. Jane Moore Howe, now a great-grandmother, is thrilled to introduce Amelia's adventures to a new generation.